THE
BIG WIN

ISLAND ADVENTURES

THE
BIG WIN

BOOK 2

AN UNOFFICIAL NOVEL FOR FANS OF ANIMAL CROSSING

WINTER MORGAN

Sky Pony Press
New York

Sky Pony Press books may be purchased in bulk at special discounts for sales promotion, corporate gifts, fund-raising, or educational purposes. Special editions can also be created to specifications. For details, contact the Special Sales Department, Sky Pony Press, 307 West 36th Street, 11th Floor, New York, NY 10018 or info@skyhorsepublishing.com.

Sky Pony® is a registered trademark of Skyhorse Publishing, Inc.®, a Delaware corporation.

Visit our website at www.skyponypress.com.

10 9 8 7 6 5 4 3 2 1

Cover design by Kai Texel
Cover artwork by Grace Sandford

Print ISBN: 978-1-5107-6528-3
E-Book ISBN: 978-1-5107-6578-8

Printed in the United States of America

TABLE OF CONTENTS

CHAPTER 1

MINOR CATASTROPHES

It was exactly two weeks until the birthday of Alana's good friend, Lars the pig. Alana was counting down the days, because she was secretly planning a big surprise party for Lars along with their other friends, Happy the hamster and Carl the chicken. Although Lars's birthday was still a few weeks away, Alana was giving him a colorful hammock she had purchased from Tick and Tock's shop. She believed if she gave him an early birthday present today, he'd never suspect she was planning anything for his birthday, especially not a surprise party.

Alana carried the hammock and headed toward Lars's house. She wanted to place the hammock between the large apple trees on the side of his home. As she approached Lars's house, she passed by her raccoon friends Tick and Tock outside the shop. They were chatting with a hedgehog who stood in front of a cart full of clothing. Sometimes it was weird being the only person on an island full of animals.

"Alana," Tick called out, "come here."

Alana walked over. "Hi, I can't stay long. I wanted to give Lars this colorful hammock."

"You're a good friend," Tock said with a smile.

"Before you go, I wanted you to meet my friend Avis. She sells clothes that you might like," Tick said, pointing to Avis's cart, which was filled with pastel T-shirts, knit hats, floral dresses, blue jeans, and an assortment of shorts.

Alana took a closer look at the clothes. "I love this shirt," Alana said as she pointed to a pink shirt hanging on the side of the cart. "How much is it?"

"Five hundred bells," Avis said.

Alana pulled five hundred bells from her pocket and handed it to Avis. "I'd like to buy the shirt."

"Do you want to try it on first? If you do, you can go into Tick and Tock's shop and see how it fits," suggested Avis.

"Good idea," Alana said, then paused. "You know, I also want to try on the blue dress. It's my friend Lars's birthday in a couple of weeks and we are planning a surprise party, and this would be the perfect dress to wear to the party."

Tick said, "You have to stop mentioning the surprise party or it won't be a surprise for long."

Alana laughed. She couldn't help mentioning the party. In fact, she had been avoiding Lars because she thought she'd let it slip, and she knew Lars had noticed. Alana hoped giving Lars the hammock would make up for avoiding him for the past few weeks. She walked into the shop and tried on the dress. She looked at herself in the mirror. The dress fit perfectly, and she had a pink floral hair clip that she thought would look great with it. Alana headed over to Avis with the two garments in hand. "I will take both of them," she said with a smile.

Avis thanked her and said, "I'm hoping to open a shop on Furtopia. Once I do, I will have all sorts of dresses, pants, and many accessories at my tailor shop."

"Wow!" Alana exclaimed. She imagined stopping by the shop to purchase new clothes. "I hope the store opens soon."

"Me too," Avis said. "Nice meeting you."

As Alana continued on to Lars's house with the colorful hammock in hand, Happy stopped her.

"Did you hear the news?" Happy asked.

"What news? I haven't heard anything new," Alana replied.

"Oh good! I love being the first to break a story." Happy clapped her hands with excitement. "There's going to be a new store opening on Furtopia. A clothing store run by the sweetest hedgehog named Avis. I believe she wants to open it with her twin sister Tavis."

Alana didn't have the heart to tell Happy that she already knew about the shop, but she didn't know about the twin sister.

"That's so exciting," Alana said. "You can get a new outfit there for Lars's party."

"Yes, and so can you!"

Alana didn't want to lie, so she said, "I actually just bought something for Lars's party from Avis's cart."

"Then you did know about the shop?" Happy questioned.

"Well, kind of. I didn't know she had a twin sister or that the store is actually going to open," Alana explained.

"I'm just so glad it will open soon," said Happy. "I love shopping. I'm already in the middle of crafting a large wardrobe for all the clothes I'm going to buy from the new shop."

"I can't wait to see it," said Alana.

"Why don't you come over for dinner tonight?"

Alana accepted the dinner invitation and then excused herself and sprinted toward Lars's house. When she reached the house, she saw Lars lying on a colorful hammock, sipping a glass of cherry juice. She quickly hid the hammock she was carrying.

"Lars," Alana remarked, "I love the new hammock."

"Thank you. My friend Janey gave it to me." Lars sat up and the hammock swung, making him almost fall to the ground. He steadied himself and climbed out of the hammock.

"Janey?" questioned Alana.

Lars said, "Yes, she's an old friend. She is visiting Furtopia."

Janey walked out of Lars's house. She was a purple cat with pink ears. She wore a red dress with large white flowers stitched on it.

"Nice to meet you," Janey said and hugged Alana.

"It's also nice to meet you." Alana wanted to say that she had heard all about Janey, but she hadn't. Lars had never mentioned her.

"Lars wants to show me around Furtopia. Do you want to join us?" Janey asked Alana.

"I'd love that. I'm not sure if Lars mentioned this, but I'm the island manager."

"He didn't, but that sounds like a cool job," Janey said as Lars led them to the beach.

"The last island I lived on was totally inadequate," Lars said as he pointed out the flowers and cherry trees. "I'm so glad that I moved to Furtopia. It was the best decision I ever made."

Janey pointed at the garden and pond by the museum. "This is truly a charming island. I'd love to check out the museum."

"It's wonderful," said Lars. "Feathers the owl runs the museum and he is so knowledgeable."

Feathers walked down the steps of the majestic museum and called to his friends. "Would you like to come in? I am working on a new exhibit I'd love for you to see."

"Yes," Alana said, and the group joined Feathers on the steps.

Feathers was so excited and spoke so fast that the group had a hard time understanding him. He led them to an empty tank. "I want to have a shark tank," he said.

"That would be awesome," said Alana. "How will you get sharks?"

"I've caught sharks before. In fact, I have one with me," Janey said. She pulled a shark out of her pocket and handed it to Feathers. "I'd love to donate it to this exhibit and place the first shark in the shark tank."

"This is amazing!" exclaimed Feathers. "I'm sorry I was so distracted by my new exhibit that I didn't properly introduce myself. My name is Feathers, and you are?"

"I'm Janey and I'm moving to Furtopia," she said.

"Janey is my best friend," explained Lars. "I've known her for years. I'm so glad she decided to move to Furtopia. I know she is going to be happy here."

Alana was upset. She thought Janey was just visiting Furtopia and now it turns out that Janey is going to stay. Since Lars moved to Furtopia, Alana had spent every day with him, and she thought of him as her best friend. She didn't want Janey moving here and taking away her best friend. She didn't know what do to, so she smiled and said, "If you're staying, I guess we should pick out a house for you."

CHAPTER 2

GONE FISHING

Alana walked along the shore with Lars and Janey. Janey paused by the coconut tree.

"Coconuts." Janey smiled. "I love coconuts." She shook the tree and picked the coconut that dropped on the ground, offering some to Lars, but not to Alana. Lars didn't seem to notice.

"Isn't this island lovely?" Lars asked. "I'm so glad you're moving here."

"Me too," Janey said.

"Aren't you going to miss the place you lived in before?" Alana questioned.

"Ever since Lars left ages ago to explore other islands, it's been so boring. I don't think I'll miss it. I can already tell that I love Furtopia. I just have to figure out the best spot to build my home," Janey said, staring out at the sea.

Happy was jogging by and stopped to introduce herself to Janey. Janey stood staring at the sea as she spoke to Happy. "It's nice to meet you. I'm sorry I'm distracted. I love to fish, and I noticed a school of fish swimming beneath the surface. I want to go fishing."

Janey pulled out her fishing rod and cast the reel into the sea. Within seconds, she had caught three sea bass. Alana didn't even know someone could catch a fish that quickly. Janey was an expert.

"Wow," Alana exclaimed, "you can really fish. I'm impressed."

"The water is crowded with fish today, so it's not as impressive as it looks. Do you have a rod on you? If so, you should join me."

Alana pulled out her old fishing rod, the one that she had used to get a koi fish that was on display at the museum. Although Alana had caught a koi and a coelacanth, she was still learning how to fish, and she hadn't caught many. Alana watched as Janey reeled in fish after fish from her line, while she, herself, didn't catch a single one.

"I don't know what I'm doing wrong. I'm still a bit new at this," Alana said. "Janey, can you help me?"

Janey put down her fishing rod and helped Alana. "Why don't you move the rod to the right?"

Alana moved the rod to the right, and she felt a tug. She reeled in a sea bass. "Thanks," Alana said. Perhaps having Janey on Furtopia wouldn't be as bad as she had imagined.

Janey said, "In two weeks, my friend D. J. is hosting a series of fishing tournaments on various islands. I was thinking of asking him to host one on Furtopia. Isn't that a great idea?"

Alana thought about the last contest she had participated in, when she had become fixated on Furtopia winning the Prettiest Island Award. Furtopia won and the prize was a private J. J. Swooner concert. The concert was magical and memorable, but the process of preparing for the contest had turned Alana into a hyper-focused person who didn't have time for anything else but trying to win the contest. Ever since Furtopia was awarded the Prettiest Island Award, Alana had been more relaxed. She spent time crafting, planting, and spending lazy days with her friends. She wasn't sure she wanted to participate in this fishing tournament, because she worried she'd go back to her old ways.

"I'm not sure Furtopia is the right place for the tournament," Alana explained. "I don't think anybody would sign up."

"Are you crazy? I'd sign up! That fishing tournament sounds like the best idea ever!" Happy exclaimed. "I love fishing!"

Carl walked over to the beach. "Hi guys. Are you fishing?"

"Yes," said Janey as she introduced herself. "I was just telling Alana about a fishing tournament that is happening on Furtopia in a few weeks."

"Really? I'd sign up," Carl remarked with a yawn. "I don't mind fishing because it doesn't require too much movement."

Alana wasn't sure how the fishing tournament went from a possibility to an actual event. She felt as if Janey was trying to take over Furtopia. Didn't Janey realize that Alana was the manager of the island? Didn't Janey realize that Lars was her best friend?

"My friend D. J. will be so excited to host the tournament here," said Janey.

"What are the prizes?" asked Alana.

"You win trophies and you can also sell the fish you caught to either D. J. or a shop owner on the island, and they will give you lots of bells for the winning fish," Janey replied.

Happy grabbed Alana's arm. "Oh my gosh! Think of all the clothes we can buy from Avis and Tavis's shop with those bells. We will be the most fashionable folks on Furtopia. Maybe we can buy matching outfits. Isn't that a great idea, Alana?"

Alana needed more bells. She wanted to splurge when the new tailor shop opened, so she agreed to participate in the contest.

"This is awesome! Let's practice now," Janey suggested. "In the tournament, we are timed and whoever catches the most fish within the allotted time is declared the winner."

"A practice contest? I'm in!" Happy got out her rod.

Lars and Carl took out their rods too. Janey asked, "Is everybody ready?"

Everyone cast their reels and Janey called out, "One. Two. Three. Go!"

Alana watched as her friends caught fish after fish, while she couldn't even seem to get a nibble. When she finally felt a tug, she reeled it in and found an old clock on her hook. She put it in the sand. When the contest was over, everybody gathered and enthusiastically showed off their piles of fish. Alana had the smallest pile of the bunch. She had caught three fish and an old broken clock.

"Does the clock count?" she joked.

"No," Janey replied coldly, as she counted everyone's catches and declared herself the winner.

"We should sell these fish to Tick and Tock," Happy suggested. "Then we can go to Avis's cart and buy some clothes."

Everyone chatted about their best strategies for catching the most fish. Lars had come in second place and was explaining that he likes to walk along the shoreline when he fishes because when you move spots, you catch more fish.

Carl remarked, "I think moving is overrated. I just stay in one place and it works out fine. I only caught one less fish than you did."

Happy added, "I don't care if I win the contest. I just want to get bells, so I can buy clothes. I am almost done with the new wardrobe that I am building by myself and I can't wait to fill it."

"Wow, you're building your own wardrobe? I'd love to see it," Janey said.

"You can come over to my house after we go to the shop," Happy suggested.

"I'd love to, but I have to find a place to build a home," Janey explained.

"Build one next to mine. We can be neighbors," Happy told her.

"Maybe I will," Janey said.

"I'm so glad you've decided to move to our island," Happy said. "I bet we're going to be best friends. We should buy matching outfits from Avis's cart."

Alana trailed behind as she listened to her friends talk. She carried her three fish and the old broken clock, and when she took a detour and went home instead of to Tick and Tock's shop, nobody seemed to notice.

CHAPTER 3

THE OTHER SIDE
OF THE ISLAND

Where did you go?" Lars asked as he climbed the stairs to Alana's porch.

Alana was surprised they had come to visit. She had watched Lars and Janey walk away after the fishing practice and not even look back to see where she was, and Alana wasn't ready to talk to them. After she left them, she had spent the afternoon on her porch swing listening to J. J. Swooner songs on her tape deck.

"I love J. J. Swooner," Janey remarked.

Alana didn't reply, just hummed along to the song.

"What happened to you?" Lars asked.

She couldn't continue with the silent treatment. She was too mature for those tactics, so she confessed, "I didn't really have anything to sell. I'm not that great at fishing."

"You have a few weeks to prepare for the tournament," Janey said.

"I'm not signing up."

"Alana, you have to sign up. I told my friend D. J. I have everyone onboard," Janey explained.

"Well you don't have me," Alana said, raising the volume on her tape deck to drown out Janey's voice.

Lars shut the tape deck off. "Alana, are you upset with me? For the past two weeks, you have been avoiding me. I always come by to chat with you, but you tell me you're busy. What's wrong?"

"I don't have any problem with you." Alana didn't want Lars knowing the real reason she was avoiding him. Happy, Carl, and Alana had been working tirelessly on the surprise party and she wasn't about to spill the beans. She excused herself, went inside her home, and returned with a colorful hammock in her hands. She said, "This was a gift I bought for you. It was an early birthday present. When I brought it over, I saw Janey had already given you one and it made me feel bad."

"That is so thoughtful. Why don't you keep it and we can have matching hammocks? Or you can give the hammock to Happy?" Lars suggested.

Janey changed the subject. "Weren't you supposed to help me find a new home? Lars said that you're the housing expert."

"I thought Happy wanted you to be her neighbor," Alana said.

"There isn't enough room by her house. I want to be in a secluded location. I like my privacy," Janey explained.

Alana couldn't believe the words that fell out of her own mouth. "I have a great place where you can be close to all of us, but still have lots of space. Let me show you." She sprinted through the grassy meadow and over the bridge to the well-manicured but desolate and undeveloped section of Furtopia.

"What about here?" She pointed to an empty patch of land surrounded by cherry and apple trees and colorful flowers.

"This might work," Janey said as she explored the potential spot for her new home.

"You will be right across the bridge from us," Lars remarked. "This is truly ideal. What a fabulous idea, Alana. I knew you'd think of something good."

"There are lots of designs for wooden homes," Alana explained. "We should talk to Wayne because he has a catalog of potential homes we can purchase for you. He has lots of connections in construction."

"It's happening! I'm going to stay on Furtopia!" Janey exclaimed as she followed Alana and Lars across the bridge.

Before they reached Tick and Tock's store, they spotted a new shop near the Resident Life building. Avis was standing in front of it, and Happy was chatting away.

"Is this the new shop?" asked Alana.

"It will be soon," Avis said with a smile. "When my sister arrives, we will put the finishing touches on it and then we will have our grand opening."

"I can't wait to start shopping. Is it possible I can get a sneak peek?" Happy asked. "I think I'm a valued customer. I did buy almost everything from your cart."

"You have shopped more than most, and you're definitely a valued customer," said Avis, "but I'm sorry that I can't let anyone in the shop before the grand opening."

Alana was concerned about Happy's recent shopping excursion. She questioned whether Happy had really bought most of the items on Avis's cart, or was she exaggerating? Alana wondered how Happy had gotten all those bells. If she had bought a bunch of clothes, she would have needed many bells.

Just as Alana was about to ask, Happy pointed at a balloon floating above them. Before anybody else had a chance to pop the balloon and claim the wrapped gift attached to the balloon's string, Happy had already hit it with her slingshot. She frantically opened the box. "Yes!" Happy exclaimed. "More bells!"

Happy handed the bells she had just pulled from the box to Avis. "I know I still owe you more bells, and I am going to earn some now." Happy raced off before Alana had a chance to talk to her.

Alana was worried about Happy, and she decided to bring up her concerns at their dinner that night. But right now she had to focus on finding the best house for Janey.

Wayne greeted them as they entered the store.

"We're looking for a home for Janey," Alana announced.

"Wow, this island is filling up rather quickly. How nice," Wayne remarked.

Tick and Tock were behind the counter and Wayne instructed them to take out the catalog of new homes.

Janey flipped through the pages and stopped when she saw a small wooden house with a large porch. "This is the house that I want."

"Great," Wayne said. "It's in stock and we can build it today."

The gang walked to the area Janey had chosen for her home. It was near the bridge, but far enough away that it felt like a desert island. When the building was completed, she invited everyone into the house.

"I'm going to have a housewarming party tonight," Janey said. "We can have a bonfire and sing songs. It will be so nice. I want to invite everyone."

"I'm supposed to have dinner with Happy," Alana said.

"Come after dinner. This is going to be the best party Furtopia has ever experienced," Janey announced.

"Let's tell Carl about it," Lars said.

Janey and Lars ran off again without waiting for Alana. Before they were out of earshot, Alana called out to them. "Wait," she shouted.

Janey turned around. "Aren't you coming, Alana?"

"Can you come back here for a minute?" asked Alana.

Janey and Lars walked back to the house, and Alana pulled the colorful hammock from her inventory.

"I want you to have the hammock," Alana said as she handed the hammock to Janey.

Lars and Janey placed the hammock between the two cherry trees next to Janey's house. Janey said, "Thank you so much for this great housewarming gift. Alana, you should be the first one to lie in the hammock."

Alana climbed into the hammock and looked up at the sun, which was setting. She thought about Janey and realized that having more residents on the island was a good thing. Alana understood that Lars could have two best friends and that she would have to learn to share.

CHAPTER 4

BIRTHDAY PLANS

The first thing Happy did when she invited Alana into her home was show off the wardrobe she had crafted.

"Isn't this nice?" Happy asked. "It took me a long time to build it."

"Wow, I can't you believe you built this yourself! It's enormous and so ornate," Alana said as she eyed the floral design on the woodwork.

Happy opened the door to the wardrobe. "Look inside. It's almost full."

Alana marveled at the collection of dresses, skirts, workout clothes, pants, and accessories that filled the closet. Although Happy had just completed the wardrobe, it was packed with items.

"I think you have to build a second wardrobe. I didn't know you had all these clothes."

Happy laughed. "I know! In fact, I am going to build a second one after I'm done preparing for the fishing competition. I know once Avis opens the new store with her sister Tavis, I will be a regular there. I definitely need more space for all the clothes I plan on buying."

"Why do you need so many clothes?" Alana asked. But Happy didn't respond. There was a knock on the door, and Happy rushed to answer it.

"Carl!" Happy exclaimed. "I'm so happy you could make it."

"I'm glad Happy is happy," Carl joked.

"You're so funny!" Happy laughed. "I'm excited that you're here. Now we can go over the birthday party plans. This is going to the best birthday party ever on Furtopia," Happy said.

"It will be the first," Carl reminded her.

"That's why it will be the best," she explained. Happy invited Carl and Alana to sit at the dining room table. She placed a large salad and a plate of fish in front of them. "I hope you guys like fish. I was practicing for the competition and I was able to catch six fish in less than two minutes."

"Really?" Carl said. "That's amazing. I was practicing, but I could only get four fish."

"Has everybody been practicing for the competition? I thought we were busy planning Lars's birthday party," Alana remarked, as her competitive side began to resurface.

"Of course," Happy said. "This is a big deal. I want to win. I already cleared a space on my nightstand for my trophy. I want to wake up every morning and be reminded of the day I won the fishing competition."

"Don't you think you're being a little too confident?"

Carl asked Happy. "Janey is excellent at fishing, and I think she might win."

"Practice makes perfect, and I will be practicing a lot," Happy said. "So I'm hopeful I will win."

Alana didn't want to talk about the fishing competition, because it made her feel very insecure. She wasn't able to catch a lot of fish in a short period of time, and she feared coming in last place. Alana reminded her friends, "Aren't we here to discuss the party?"

"Yes!" Happy exclaimed as she the rattled off a list of items they would need for the party, including a piñata, cupcakes, party poppers, and many other items.

"We have to find a good way to surprise Lars," Carl said.

As they came up with inventive ways to surprise Lars, there was another knock at the door. Happy ran to the door and Janey was there. Alana was shocked. She didn't expect Janey to be at the dinner.

Happy exclaimed, "Janey! I'm so glad you could make it. I know you have your housewarming party later. We are so excited to celebrate with you tonight. Since you obviously love throwing parties, can you help us plan one for Lars?"

"Of course," Janey said as she sat down at the table and helped herself to a large portion of fish. "How about throwing a pool party?"

"There isn't a pool on Furtopia," Alana explained.

"Why don't we build one on my side of the island? Since it's not very developed, Lars would never find it," Janey said as she stuffed her face with fish and began to chew.

Alana had seen pools in the catalog Tick and Tock had on display in their shop. She spent many days perusing the pages of the catalog and dreaming about all the items she could buy. Alana had always wanted a pool, but they were very expensive, and she knew that it would take a long time to collect enough bells to purchase one.

"Alana, you can buy him a pool," Happy suggested. "That could be your present."

"I don't have enough bells to buy a pool," she replied.

"Well, then you will have to save up," Happy instructed.

"Do you have enough time to save up that many bells? Lars's party is two weeks away," Carl yawned. "It seems like an awfully hard thing to do. I can't imagine how many items you'd have to sell to Tick and Tock to get that many bells."

Alana wanted to sprint around the island trying to find money rocks. She also wanted to wait outside her door to shoot down any balloons with presents attached. Some of the presents were filled with bells. However, she knew these weren't the best strategies. If she won the fishing competition, maybe she'd win enough bells to purchase the pool. Then Alana had an idea.

"Maybe we can all buy the pool together. If we pool our bells together," Alana laughed as she made the pun, "we might be able to buy it."

"That's a great idea," Happy exclaimed. "Except I don't have any bells left. I spent them all on clothing and the kit to build the wardrobe."

"I have some bells," Carl said as he pulled them out of his pocket. He placed the bells on the table and began counting.

Janey looked at the bells Carl stacked on the table and said, "It doesn't look like you have enough bells."

"Three hundred," Carl announced.

"A pool costs a lot more," Alana said.

"Well, it's a start," Carl said, "and I'm more than happy to donate these bells to the pool fund."

"Thank you," Alana said.

Janey reminded them, "I have my party soon, so I can't stay. I'm sorry I don't have any bells to donate, but I will try to earn some bells in the next couple of weeks and will be glad to donate those. If I win the competition, I will donate my winnings, and then I'm sure we'll have enough bells to pay for the pool."

"I'm going to win the fishing competition," Happy declared.

"Well, if you do, you should use your winnings to buy the pool," Janey instructed Happy.

Happy stared at her wardrobe as she replied, "I can donate a small portion, but I need my bells to buy clothes. I hear the new tailor shop is opening tomorrow, and I can't wait."

"I think the pool is a priority," Janey said as she walked out of Happy's house.

When she left, Happy asked Carl and Alana, "Do you think we have to throw a pool party?"

"I like pools," Carl said. "I'm a fan of still water. I find the ocean waves to be so tiring."

"I think it's expensive," said Alana, "but a great idea. We can all use the pool and I know Lars would be so happy to have a pool party. I am just worried we won't get enough bells in time."

"Me too," Happy said.

CHAPTER 5

HOUSEWARMING PARTY

Alana hoped Happy wouldn't spill the beans about the pool party. Happy spent the entire walk over to Janey's house talking about how she wished she had more bells to donate to the pool fund.

"I think the pool is the best idea ever. I just wish it wasn't so expensive," Happy said for the hundredth time that night.

"Don't worry about it, Happy. Alana is resourceful and will help us get the bells," Carl said, and then added, "I hope this party doesn't run too late. I'm tired and I don't think I'll be able to stay up."

As they crossed the bridge to Janey's side of the island, Alana stopped and looked up at the stars. It was a gorgeous night without a cloud in the sky. Alana could make out some constellations. She remembered learning about astronomy in her science class. The teacher had told the class that visible stars are bigger than the sun. Alana had questioned whether this was true, but she looked it up: It was. As they walked toward Janey's house, Alana stared at the moon and the stars lighting up the night sky. There was another light off in the distance and the faint smell of smoke.

"I think they have a bonfire," Happy said as she sprinted toward the party. "Sorry," she called out as she looked back, "I have to get some cardio in. I will see you guys at the party."

Carl and Alana followed the sound of people's voices, the music, and the light from the bonfire. When they arrived at the party, they found Lars and Janey dancing. Tick, Tock, Wayne, and Feathers were crowded around the bonfire telling stories. Happy was running laps around Janey's backyard. Carl spotted the empty hammock and crawled into it.

"I'm going to take a nap," he told Alana, "so can you ask the others to keep it down?"

"I can't do that," Alana explained. "This is a party. You're just going to have to sleep through all the noise."

"Oh well," Carl sighed, "I guess I'll manage."

Alana noticed a bear dancing alongside Janey and Lars. She walked over and introduced herself. "I'm Alana," she said as she shook the bear's paw.

Although this bear was dressed in jeans and a button-down shirt, the bear reminded her of Furry, her beloved teddy bear that she had since she was a baby. Furry was the inspiration for the island's name.

"I'm Bobby. I just arrived here. I used to live on Janey's old island. She told me about Furtopia and how lovely it is, and I decided to move here."

"Where are you going to live?" Alana asked.

"I am going to be Janey's neighbor, just like I was on the last island."

"That's great. It's really nice to meet you. I am so happy Furtopia is attracting new residents. I'm the island manager and I love that the island is a success."

"Janey told me all about you. She said you would be able to help me build a house. I'd love to get one tomorrow."

"I can help you find a house," Alana said.

"Thank you," Bobby said.

Alana felt like her to-do list was growing by the minute. She had to purchase a pool for Lars's party, she had to build a house for Bobby, and both of these activities would leave her with very little time to prepare for the fishing competition. Alana didn't think this was fair, especially given the fact that she wasn't very good at fishing. She didn't express these thoughts to Bobby, though. Instead, she just told him about the different types of homes he might want to choose.

As Alana and Bobby spoke, Feathers walked over and joined in their conversation. "The museum is doing quite well. Of course, it would be nice to have some new additions to the museum. You haven't donated anything in a bit."

"I'm sorry, Feathers," Alana said, "I have been busy. I promise I'll donate some items soon."

Alana added this to her seemingly never-ending list of things she had to do.

"I'd love a new fish for the museum," Feathers said.

"Okay, I was planning on fishing tomorrow and I promise to donate whatever I catch," Alana told Feathers.

Bobby said, "I hear there's going to be a fishing competition on the island in a couple of weeks."

"Yes," Alana confessed, "but I'm not very good at catching lots of fish in a short period of time. I seem to be better at catching a wide variety of fish, but not a lot of them."

"As the old saying goes, it's quality, not quantity," Feathers said.

"That's not true when it comes to winning this competition," Alana explained. "Everybody is participating, and they're all so much better than me. The other day we had a practice competition and I came in last place. I'm afraid I'm going to come in last place at the competition and I will be embarrassed."

"There's nothing wrong with coming in last place," Bobby said. "It means that you tried. You know what would be worse? If you didn't compete at all because you were afraid that you'd be in last place. I think that would be the worst."

"It's so embarrassing to be in last place," Alana said.

"I don't think it is," Feathers added. "I'm not the best fisherman in the world, but I am signing up. It seems like it's going to be fun."

"I have an idea," Bobby said. "I am a strong fisherman and I've actually taught people how to fish in the past. Would you like me to be your coach? We can start as soon as tomorrow. I was just thinking of ways I could repay you for helping me build a house, and this would be a great way."

"I'd love that. I really need a coach," Alana exclaimed.

"Great, then it's settled. I will be your coach," Bobby said.

"Don't forget to donate the first fish you catch to the museum. I want to fill up a new tank," said Feathers.

Alana joined Lars, Janey, and Happy dancing on the grass. She was thrilled that Bobby was going to be her coach. She called Bobby over to join them, and they all danced underneath the starry sky.

CHAPTER 6

GRAND OPENING

A lana awoke to Happy knocking on her door. "Alana! Alana! Alana! Wake up!" Happy called out. With a yawn and a stretch, Alana made her way from the bed to the front door. It wasn't a long distance, but Alana was exhausted. She had stayed up until the wee hours of the night dancing at Janey's housewarming party. After they finished dancing, Lars had suggested they go for a late-night swim. They went to the beach and swam for hours. After that, Alana had made her way home. She had fallen asleep in wet clothes hoping she could sleep late. Her plans were upended when Happy knocked on her door at daybreak.

"How can you be up?" Alana asked with a yawn.

"Today is the biggest day ever," Happy announced.

"The fishing competition and Lars's birthday party are a few weeks away," she said.

"No. Today Avis is opening the store with her sister Tavis. I couldn't even sleep a wink last night. All I could

31

think about were the amazing clothes I was going to buy."

Alana said, "I thought you didn't have any bells. Didn't you say that yesterday?"

"I don't have enough to donate to the pool fund because I had to put all my bells aside for this awesome day. I'm sorry my clothing budget is so high, but I just love shopping and I want to fill that amazing wardrobe."

"But what about the pool party? We all want to buy things, but we can't have a pool party without a pool."

Happy sighed. "Don't be a party pooper. You know I'll donate bells. I just want to enjoy this monumental day with my best friend. Can't you see that?"

Happy's comment made Alana feel guilty. Alana told herself that she should support Happy. This day meant a lot to her. Happy stood by Alana when she was hyper-focused on getting J. J. Swooner to play on the island. Alana reminded herself that everyone had different wants and goals.

"Okay, I will go," Alana said with a yawn, "but if you can spare any extra bells, I'd love to put them in the pool fund. If I sell some wood, fish, and fruit today, we will be on target to meet our goal, but we really can't meet it unless we all chip in."

"I totally get it and I will give you some bells, but first, shopping! I can't wait to buy new workout clothes and to see what Avis and Tavis have in their shop. I loved everything Avis had on her cart, but there wasn't much of a selection."

Alana followed behind Happy as she jogged to the new shop. The sun had just risen and there was nobody outside. Alana saw a butterfly flit past. She took out a net from her pocket and caught the butterfly.

"I think," Alana said, "while you wait for the store to open, I will gather resources from the island, like fruit and stuff I can sell when Tick and Tock's shop opens this morning. I hear they pay the best rates for fruit in the morning hours."

"Okay," Happy said, "but don't take too long. I want to walk through the doors with you. I want to enjoy this amazing moment with you by my side."

Alana didn't tell Happy that she was annoyed Happy hadn't volunteered to help Alana pick fruit and collect branches to sell.

The first tree Alana shook was an apple tree. A bunch of fresh red apples fell onto the grass, and Alana quickly picked them up. She was glad that a few branches fell beside the apples. The second tree Alana shook was a cherry tree, and only a handful of cherries landed on the grass. She shook it again, but this time nothing fell to the ground, and Alana was growing frustrated.

"Alana!" Happy called out. "Avis is here! Come back! The store is about to open!"

Alana ran back and Avis stepped outside the store. Her sister Tavis stood beside her. Avis announced, "Welcome to our tailor shop. I am so glad you are our first visitors."

Happy cheered and followed the sisters into the shop and over to a rack of pink, red, and purple dresses. She picked up a pink dress and held it against her body.

"Does this look good, Alana?"

"It does. It's a great color for you," Alana said.

"I'm going to get it! What are you buying?"

Alana didn't want to spend any bells because she wanted to use everything she had for the pool, but she couldn't resist a T-shirt with a large daisy on it and a cute baseball cap. She picked up the items. "I'm going to buy these."

"They're so cute. You made a great selection."

"Thanks," Alana said as she stared at herself in the mirror. Her two red pigtails came undone as she took the hat off.

"This is the best day, isn't it?" Happy asked.

"It is," Alana said.

"The store is open until 6 p.m. if you want to come back. We will be having cake in front of the shop at around noon to celebrate the grand opening," Avis told them.

"I'll be back for that celebration," Happy said. "I'll bring some more friends to the shop."

When Alana left the shop, she went to see Tick and Tock to sell her goods. She was upset that she only made enough bells to replenish what she had spent at the new tailor shop. Happy waited for Alana outside Tick and Tock's shop.

"Are you going to come back to the tailor shop at noon?" Happy asked.

"I don't think I can," said Alana.

"Don't you want cake?" Happy asked.

"Of course I do," Alana replied, "but I don't know if I will have time."

Alana had to gather donations for the museum, help Bobby build a house, and earn enough bells to build a pool. She hoped she could squeeze a quick break in for a slice of cake.

"I think you should find the time," Happy said. "Cake is awesome."

"I think you're right," Alana said as she left to accomplish the first item on her to-do list.

CHAPTER 7

THE COACH

Alana was fishing in the deep part of the river, hoping to catch a sturgeon, which appeared in the water around September. She stood on the bridge holding a fishing rod and leaning over the railing to see why no fish were taking the bait. The summer was winding down and September had just started, and although it was probably too early in the season to catch a sturgeon, Alana was going to try. She knew if she caught one sturgeon, she'd be able to cross the museum donation off her to-do list.

There was a cool breeze blowing Alana's red pigtails. It was nice to feel the brisk air on her skin, but she was also sad that this was a sign summer was coming to an end. She hadn't snorkeled as much as she had hoped, and she was going to miss bonfires and lazy beach days. As Alana waited for a bite, she thought of all the fun things she could do in the winter to make herself look forward to the colder months. She loved ice skating and making snowmen and snow forts, and she also liked hot chocolate. As she tried to come up with more fun winter activities, Bobby called out to her. He crossed the bridge and stopped next to Alana as she fished.

"Have you caught anything?" he asked.

She clutched the fishing rod with one hand and pointed to the bucket with another. "Nope. See? The bucket is empty. I wonder if I'd have better luck at the beach."

"I can help you," Bobby said. "I did promise I could coach you, right? So let's start the coaching now."

"I'm not practicing for the competition right now. I'm trying to catch a sturgeon that Feathers can display in the museum. I know it's a rare fish. Do you think that's impossible?"

"It's hard, but not impossible," Bobby said.

"I've been here a pretty long time, and I still haven't caught anything."

"May I borrow the rod?" Bobby asked.

"Of course. If you want to be my coach, I am ready for the first lesson."

"A coach is a bit different than a teacher. I know you understand how to fish, so I'm not here to teach you but to get you in shape for the competition," Bobby explained. He reeled in the line, removed the bait from the hook, and handed it to Alana. "I have some bait that might work better."

He pulled out bait from his pocket and attached it to the hook. He cast the reel into the deep, calm, murky river and within seconds he reeled in a fish with a dark blue head, an almost transparent turquoise trunk, and a pale tail.

"Oh my! Is that a rare fish?" Alana asked.

"It's a pale chub. It's very common. Have you not been on Furtopia very long?"

"No, I just arrived this summer. As you can see from Janey's part of the island, we are still developing Furtopia."

"That explains why you're not the best fisherman. It takes a while to learn how to fish well, and you can't really rush the process. I am going to help you as much as I can, but you have to understand that everyone else in the competition has been fishing a lot longer than you."

"I get it," Alana said as she watched Bobby reel in a second pale chub. "Do you think Feathers would want a pale chub for the museum?" Alana asked.

Bobby said, "You can offer it to him, but let's fish a bit longer and see if we can find a sturgeon. The key to becoming a good fisherman is patience. There were times on my old island when I would wait for hours before I caught a fish."

"I can't do that at the competition. If I did, I'd be the person who came in last, and I don't want that."

"There's always someone who comes in last. I don't think you should focus on that at all. I think you should focus on trying to be a better fisherman," Bobby said as he handed the rod back to Alana. "Now you try to fish. Just remember to cast the line at an angle, and you can use my bait."

Alana placed Bobby's bait on the hook and cast the reel into the water. It seemed like she had been waiting for an hour before she felt something tug on her line. Alana reeled in the line, but there wasn't a fish attached. An old tire dangled from the end of the line. Tears streamed down her cheeks.

Bobby said, "I went to the museum yesterday and saw a gorgeous coelacanth. Are you the one who caught it?"

"Yes," Alana replied with a sniffle.

"It took me a full year to catch that rare fish. You have no idea how many rainy nights I woke up in the middle of a storm, put on my rain slicker and rain boots, went fishing for a coelacanth, and didn't catch anything. I was ready to give up when I finally caught one."

"Have you ever gotten trash like a boot or a tire?" Alana asked. "I feel like I get them all the time. I always think I have a big fish at the end of the reel and get so upset when I see it's not a fish at all."

"Alana, you've only been on Furtopia since the summer. I've been living on these islands for years. You can't say that you get a lot of trash, because this is only the beginning for you. Yes, you will get a lot of trash when you fish, because that's what happens. However, sometimes you catch a big rare fish. If you give up, you know what you will catch?"

"Nothing," Alana replied.

"That's correct." Bobby smiled. "And catching nothing is a lot worse than reeling in the occasional tire or other rubbish that is found in the water."

"I guess you're right." Alana placed the tire on the wooden bridge and cast her reel back in the water.

"Just be patient and you will catch something."

Alana hummed a J. J. Swooner song as she looked down at the water, hoping she would get a bite, but the river seemed empty of fish. She wanted to pull the fishing rod out of the water and give up. "Maybe we should take a break from fishing and help you build a house?" Alana suggested.

"Just wait," Bobby said as he looked at the river.

Alana screamed, "I feel a pull on the line! I feel a pull!"

"Reel it in," Bobby said.

Alana reeled in the line and saw a pale chub on the hook. "Wow, I also got a pale chub."

"See? I knew you'd get something."

She pulled the fish off the hook, placed it in the bucket, and cast the line back in the water. While she waited for another bite, a voice called out to her.

"Are you fishing? It's so early," Carl said as he approached the bridge.

"You're also up early," remarked Alana.

"I fell asleep on Janey's hammock during the start of the housewarming party and I just woke up," Carl confessed.

"I was shocked you could sleep through all the noise," Bobby said. "We were dancing and laughing. I'm sorry you missed out on that."

"I'm not. It sounds so exhausting," Carl said with a yawn. "I need to go home now and rest. I didn't get a proper sleep last night. Sleeping on a hammock isn't as good as sleeping on a bed."

There was a heavy tug on the line and Alana screamed, "I think I have one!"

"Reel it in," Bobby said.

A sturgeon was hanging from the hook. "I did it! I can't wait to tell Feathers!"

"Great job!" Bobby exclaimed.

"I don't know where you guys get your energy," Carl said and walked away.

"I'm so glad you're my coach, Bobby."

"I don't want to get credit for anything. You're the one who is doing all the work."

"Now that I've crossed the museum donation off my list, let's build you a house," Alana said as she placed the sturgeon in the bucket.

"Great, but you should bring the sturgeon to Feathers before we go house shopping."

The two new friends walked toward the museum. Alana proudly carried the bucket with her fresh catches.

CHAPTER 8

ANOTHER ESCAPE

F eathers?" Alana called as she stood on the museum steps and knocked on the large wooden doors. The door was locked, and he wasn't answering. Alana looked over at Bobby. "I wonder where Feathers is. Maybe he's at the store."

"It's almost noon," Bobby said. "Isn't there a party for Avis's new store at noon?"

"Oh yes!" Alana said. "I almost forgot. Happy wanted to meet me there."

"We should go to the center of town and stop by the grand opening," Bobby replied. "I'm curious to see what's in the store. I need some workout clothes. I can't go running in jeans and a button-down shirt."

Alana was taken aback when Bobby referred to the area that housed the Resident Life building, Tick and Tock's shop, and Avis and Tavis's shop as "the center of town." When Alana arrived on Furtopia, there was only a Resident Life tent, and now the island had two stores and a museum. She was happy that Furtopia was becoming so developed.

As they made their way toward the shop, Bobby asked, "Are you excited to see this new store?"

Alana replied, "Happy woke me up early this morning. She wanted to be the first customer in the shop."

"Happy must love buying clothes," Bobby remarked.

Alana didn't want to gossip, but she was worried about Happy. Happy seemed to be buying clothes all the time and Alana wondered why Happy needed so many clothes when she was only one hamster.

"She does," Alana said, as she spotted Happy standing in front of the store along with Janey, Lars, Feathers, Wayne, Tick, and Tock. Avis and Tavis stood by the cake, which was on a table next to an apple tree.

"Great! They're here!" Happy called out.

Avis made a speech thanking everyone for coming. Everyone applauded, and then her sister Tavis cut the cake. Alana thanked Tavis as she handed her a slice of cake. Feathers walked over.

"What's in the bucket?" Feathers asked.

"I caught a sturgeon. I was about to donate it to the museum."

"This is the best news ever!" Feathers exclaimed. "I must get back to the museum and place the sturgeon in the water. You are such a good friend, Alana. The museum would be empty without you."

"Thanks," Alana blushed.

Feathers picked up the bucket and went back to the museum, and Alana was glad to cross one item off her to-do list. She saw Wayne walking into the Resident Life building and followed him in. She wanted to talk to him about trying to find a way to finance the pool.

"I was thinking of building a pool," she explained to Wayne. "Everyone thought it would be nice to have a pool party for Lars's birthday."

"That sounds like a good idea," Wayne said. "I like that the residents of Furtopia love to throw parties, don't you?"

"Yes," she replied, "but I'm in charge of constructing both Bobby's new home and the pool, and I'm afraid I don't have enough bells."

"Do you have anything to sell? You can always go to Tick and Tock's store and sell goods. I know they are paying a lot for oranges."

"Furtopia only has cherries and apples," Alana reminded him.

"I think you should use your miles to go on another excursion to a desert island. I'm sure on just one of those trips you'll be able to gather enough items to sell, and you'll have enough bells to cover both the new house and the pool. Also, you'll be able to populate Furtopia with new trees and flowers."

Alana remembered the last time she took a trip to another island. That time she was escaping the island because she thought Happy and Carl didn't like her. She remembered meeting Lars on the island and shaking the apple and coconut trees and bringing back the fruit to plant trees on Furtopia. She wondered whether she had enough time to visit an island, because she didn't want to fall behind in her training. She really didn't want to come in last place in the fishing competition.

"I guess I can, but when would I go?" Alana asked Wayne.

"I have a seaplane on the dock that's ready to go. You ready?" Wayne asked.

Alana said yes and walked alongside Wayne toward the dock. Tick and Tock were on the seaplane and welcomed her aboard. She looked out the window and watched Furtopia grow smaller as they flew further into the blue skies. The plane ride didn't take very long and soon they were landing on the sea. Tick opened the door to the plane and helped Alana climb onto the dock.

"Oranges!" Alana exclaimed as she looked at the lush island filled with orange trees. Alana sprinted from the pier and shook all the orange trees filling her pockets with the juicy fruit. She also gathered all the branches that fell to the ground. Alana wanted to gather as many goods as fast as she could. She sprinted around the island in search of a pond, but the island only had a river. After filling her pockets with oranges and hardwood from the trees and fallen branches, she wondered whether she had gotten all the resources from this desert island. She hoped there would be an inhabitant, like Lars, who would tell her the secrets of the island and what would be best to sell, but there wasn't.

Alana pulled out her fishing rod and stood on the island's beach. She was patient like Bobby advised, but when the sun began to set and she hadn't gotten a bite, Alana thought she should give up and go home. She didn't want to be stuck on this island after dark. She had no place to sleep and she was tired. Just when she was about to give up, she felt a tug and reeled it in. Alana was happy to see a sea bass hanging from the hook. She placed the sea bass in her pocket and was about to walk back to the seaplane when she stumbled on a rock.

Feathers had given her a stone ax and told her to always carry it with her. He said that the stone ax is an invaluable tool for deciphering whether a rock is valuable.

"You never know what is hidden inside a rock," Feathers told her when he handed her the ax as a gift.

She thought about those words as she slammed her stone ax into the rock and saw little slivers of gold.

"I found gold!" Alana exclaimed, but there was nobody there to hear her. "I found gold!" Alana filled her pockets with gold nuggets. She spotted several more rocks on her journey back to the seaplane, and she stopped to break open each rock with her stone ax.

"Iron!" Alana yelled.

Each rock contained valuable nuggets that she could sell to Tick and Tick. The sun had set when Alana entered the seaplane, her pockets heavy with fruit, gold, iron, wood, and branches. She wondered how much she would earn for these finds and she hoped it was enough to buy a home for Bobby and a pool. As the plane approached Furtopia, Alana could see a small light in the dark sky. It looked like a bonfire. Alana couldn't wait for the plane to land, so she could join her friends beside the fire.

CHAPTER 9

CONSTRUCTION

Alana raced over to the bonfire beside Janey's house. She wanted to tell them about all the great finds she had discovered on the island, and how she could finally get the pool, but she realized that Lars was there and he couldn't know about the pool. Alana couldn't believe there was a time when she was only worried about spilling the beans about the party, and actually avoided Lars because she was afraid that she would accidentally tell him. Now she felt confident that she could keep quiet. In fact, Alana was teeming with confidence, and she felt she had earned it. In one day, she was able to catch a sturgeon for the museum and fill her pockets with gold, enabling her to buy Bobby a nice wooden house and a pool for Lars's party. She felt invincible until she remembered the fishing competition was two weeks away and she still wasn't skilled at catching a large quantity of fish in a short amount of time.

The gang sat around the bonfire singing J. J. Swooner songs. Janey said, "I wish he would come back and perform another concert."

"Me too," Bobby said.

"I think he may come back one day," Alana said. "I know when we won the contest, I was told that he does make appearances on islands if they are able to maintain the rating."

"How can we make the island prettier?" Janey asked.

"I went to another island today and picked up oranges and I'm going to plant orange trees around the island. In the morning, I'm also going to buy Bobby a house. I think both of those things will make our island's rating stay the same or go even higher, so maybe J. J. Swooner will come back in the future," Alana said.

"That would be great," Janey said. "And don't forget about the pool!"

"The pool?" Lars questioned.

Janey put her hand over her mouth. Alana wanted to joke that the cat was out of the bag, but she didn't. She just helped Janey by changing the subject. "I think Janey meant pond. She was helping me fish for koi fish in the pond. She wants me to get better at fishing. So does Bobby, and he's been the best coach. Today he helped me catch a sturgeon," Alana babbled.

"A sturgeon! That's fantastic," Lars said, and he seemed to forget about the pool.

"Yes, I donated it to the museum," Alana said, and then excused herself and went home to rest. It had been a long day and she wanted to wake up early and get started on the construction for the house, and now she knew she had to be extra careful about hiding the construction of the pool.

Alana climbed into bed and fell asleep within seconds. When she awoke, the sun was peering through her curtains. She got dressed and sprinted toward Tick and Tock's shop. As she approached the store, she saw Happy walking out of the tailor shop.

"You're up early," Happy remarked.

"I have to start building Bobby's home. He has been staying with Janey and he wants to get his own place. Have you been shopping?"

"I was just doing my morning cardio and I thought I'd stop in and say hi to Avis and Tavis. I did buy a headband. You know how much I like to wear them when I do my daily jogs," Happy replied. Alana nodded.

She went into Tick and Tock's shop and placed the pile of gold nuggets on the counter.

"How much can I get for this?" she asked.

"Gold nuggets," Tick said as he put on a monocle and carefully inspected the gold. "These are very rare and are worth lots of bells."

"I also have iron nuggets," Alana said, as she pulled them from her pockets.

Tick picked up the iron nuggets. "You really outdid yourself."

"And oranges," Alana said, pulling an orange out and showed it to Tick.

Tock ran over to Alana. "We have been searching for oranges!"

"When I leave here, I'm going to plant a bunch of

orange trees around Furtopia. I am so excited to drink orange juice again."

Alana thought about the breakfasts she used to have before school and how her mother always made fresh squeezed orange juice with their juicer. She thought about September mornings in her house and the chaos of starting the new school year. Everything was different on Furtopia. She didn't have to go to school here, but there were other responsibilities. She learned how to gather valuable resources, which enabled her to build a home for Bobby and a pool for her friends. Of course, soon it would be the first frost. They didn't have a long time to enjoy the pool that year.

When Tick and Tock told Alana she had enough bells to build the house and construct the pool she let out a cheer. She left the shop and sprinted to Janey's home to tell Bobby that she needed his help choosing the home.

Bobby was so excited to get his own home that he raced to Tick and Tock's store. He chose a large wooden home with a big red door. He selected a spot near Janey's house, right on the water.

"Do you think we could put a swing in front of the house like you have?" Bobby asked.

"Yes," Alana said, "and we can also put a couple of chairs beside the water."

Once the house was built, Alana planted some orange and apple trees beside the house. Then Bobby asked Alana if she wanted to practice fishing again. "I can time you and we can see how many fish you catch. I'll fish too."

Bobby grabbed his fishing rod and Alana took hers out and they both cast their rods into the water.

"Ready. Set. Go."

Three minutes went by when he called out, "Stop!"

They looked at their buckets and counted the fish. Alana had three and Bobby had seven.

"Three isn't bad," Alana said, and then congratulated Bobby on winning the practice contest.

"You're improving, and I can teach you tricks to help you win the contest, but first we have to find a place for the new pool."

Alana wondered what tricks Bobby had and how they would help her win the competition.

CHAPTER 10

TIME TRAVEL

Alana practiced with Bobby for the next few days, but he never mentioned the tricks again, and she didn't bring it up. There were a few times when Bobby would tell Alana about various bait and the best way to angle your rod to catch more fish, but she didn't think this was what he meant when he said tricks. When he brought up the tricks, he seemed to infer that there was a secret way to win the competition. Alana was curious to hear it, but she wasn't as focused on winning anymore. She just didn't want to come in last.

One sunny morning, with a week to go before the fishing contest, Tick alerted Alana that the pool was in stock and ready to be built. Alana asked Janey where it should go and how they might go about hiding it from Lars until the day of the party, which was a little more than a week away.

"Easy," Janey said. "I won't invite Lars over to my house. I'll just find an excuse to always be on your side of the island. I will also make sure he doesn't visit

Bobby. Besides that, there's no reason to go over to my side of the island. The only other resident who comes here is Happy, and that's because she does her cardio. Bobby also jogs around here, but again, that doesn't matter because he lives here. This side of the island is very quiet. If you place the pool by the edge of the island, by the small garden I planted, I will make sure Lars doesn't see it."

Bobby helped Alana with the pool's construction, and when it was done, they both jumped in and went for a swim.

"This is so nice," Bobby said. "Now I have a spot to do laps. I do like swimming in the sea, but it's not for lap swimming. I'm so glad we have this pool."

Alana looked at the area surrounding the pool. It was just a grassy meadow, and she thought it would be nice if they created a patio with lounge chairs and tables. "I think we should build a fence around this area and then create a space for chairs and tables."

"That's a great idea," Bobby said, and then he swam another lap.

"The only problem is I don't know if I'll have enough time to build the patio and train for the competition."

Bobby stepped out of the pool and said, "I have a trick I can teach you that can help you win the competition and you won't have to practice anymore."

"I can win and I don't have to practice?" Alana asked suspiciously. "I don't think I trust this trick."

Bobby ignored Alana's question and asked, "Have you ever traveled backward or forward in time?"

"No," Alana replied with a perplexed expression. "That isn't possible."

"It is, and people do it all the time."

"Really? Why?" Alana asked.

"Sometimes someone can't wait for a holiday like Christmas or their birthday, so they move their calendar ahead to that day, so they can either celebrate it sooner or relive it if it happened already."

"I never did something like that, and I never wanted to. If you can just travel through time whenever you like, you'll have nothing to wait for. I know I'm not the most patient person, but I love having something to look forward to, and I think time travel would ruin that part of the fun."

"I understand your point, but the way we will use time travel will be a bit different. Can we try it first and then you can make up your mind?" Bobby asked.

"How? What time period are we going to travel to?"

Bobby replied, "To the future. Since you've never seen a fishing tournament, we can watch the one happening here next week and you can see everything that happens, so you feel prepared."

This seemed very logical to Alana and she agreed. "What a good idea. Let's go."

"I can't go with you," Bobby explained. "Only the island manager can time travel, but I can show you how to do it. Get your calendar and change the date."

She went to her calendar and changed the date to the day of the fishing tournament and within seconds she was standing in future Furtopia, on the day of the competition. Alana was surprised at the beautiful patio and ornate wooden fence surrounding the pool. Orange trees had sprouted around the outside of the fence. Alana could hear voices in the distance and a loudspeaker. She realized the competition must be happening at that moment, so she sprinted over to the water and hid behind a tree. She watched everyone take part in the fishing tournament. She even watched herself cast a rod into the water.

The timer went off and the gang pulled their rods from the water as a beaver named D. J. collected their buckets and counted their fish. Before they declared a winner, she pulled out her calendar and changed the date back. She didn't want to know who won the contest. In an instant she was standing by the pool, but Bobby wasn't there.

"Bobby?" Alana called out, but there was no answer. She sprinted to Janey's house, but she wasn't home either.

Alana was walking toward the bridge to go to the center of town when she spotted Lars coming over it.

"Where are you going?" Alana asked nervously. She wanted Lars to avoid that side of the island because she didn't want him to discover the new pool.

"Alana!" Lars exclaimed. "Where have you been? I was looking for you."

"I was just practicing fishing with Bobby."

"Nobody has seen Bobby either," Lars said.

"We need to find him. It's strange because I was just fishing with him and he suggested that I . . . "

Alana stopped herself. She didn't want to tell Lars about the time traveling because watching the tournament gave her an unfair advantage. Although she didn't stick around to hear who was declared the winner, she saw who caught the most fish. Alana figured if she was positioned where that player had been, she might be able to catch the most fish.

"What did he suggest?" Lars asked.

"Oh nothing," Alana replied. "I forget. It was about fishing."

"Let me know if you remember, because it might give us a clue to where he is," Lars said.

Alana still had to stop Lars from walking over the bridge to the other side of the island. "Do you want to come over for some orange juice?" Alana asked Lars. "I made fresh squeezed orange juice this morning."

"That sounds great," Lars said.

"Good, let's go now," Alana said, hoping the orange juice was still in her refrigerator. She worried that this one trip into the future had left a devastating impact on the past.

As they walked toward her house, Carl sauntered by. "Alana, you're back," Carl remarked. "There were rumors that you were eaten by a shark when you were practicing for the competition."

"Nope, I'm here," Alana said with a giggle.

"Have you seen Bobby?" Carl asked.

Alana said, "I was just with him, but he seems to have disappeared. I can find him." Alana hoped she would.

CHAPTER 11

LOST AND FOUND

Alana did find Bobby, but it took all day. She found him sitting on the beach eating a coconut.

"What happened to you?" Alana asked.

"What happened to you?" Bobby responded.

"I went to the future like you suggested, you know that." Alana was annoyed.

"Right! Of course," Bobby said. "Did it help?"

"I guess so. I felt a lot of guilt because it seemed like I was cheating, so I left before they declared the winner."

"The minute you left I regretted suggesting it," Bobby confessed. "I have been on the beach hoping you'd return safely and that traveling to the future wouldn't have a negative impact on you and the island."

"What? I didn't know time travel was bad. Then why did you tell me to travel to the future and watch the competition?" Alana asked.

"I thought it would lessen the pre-contest jitters, but I knew it was a bad idea. I was upset with myself and so I went off to figure out why I'd suggest time travel to you. I should have warned you that time travel isn't the greatest idea. If you travel too far ahead, Furtopia could suffer. If you decide to see what the island is like in a year, you might find it overrun with weeds. We aren't really meant to time travel, and I should have never suggested it," explained Bobby.

"Thanks for warning me, but I don't think I'm going to do it again. It made me feel yucky. It was so strange to hide and watch the contest. I'd much rather spend my time practicing than finding tricks to win. I think I should become a better fisherman."

"What did you see?"

"I just watched how it was set up and I saw D. J. the beaver. I didn't stick around to see who won."

"Did you get a glimpse into the buckets to see who was catching the most fish?"

Alana replied, "It seemed like everyone was catching fish, even me."

"Then, you have nothing to worry about," said Bobby.

"I know that we have a lot of work ahead of us. When I was transported to the future, I saw the patio beside the pool, and it was really nice. I know that is going to take a long time to build."

"Well, let's get that out of the way. We can go see Tick and Tock and purchase all the items you saw in the future," Bobby suggested.

They were steps from Tick and Tock's shop when Happy called out to them. She stood outside the tailor shop holding a T-shirt and pants. "Hi," Happy said.

She looked down at the shirt and pants. "I just bought these. Aren't they nice?"

"They are," Alana replied, "but your wardrobe is almost full. Why do you need all these clothes? I feel like you're at this shop every day and you need to take a break."

Happy grimaced. "Can you please mind your own business? I can buy whatever I want to if I have enough bells."

"I'm sorry," Alana said. "We were about to purchase all the furniture and a patio for the pool. Everyone has chipped in an equal amount, except for you."

"Is that what you're so upset about?" Happy pulled out some bells from her pocket and threw them at Alana. Alana stared at the glistening bells on the grass, as Happy trotted off without saying goodbye.

Bobby leaned over and picked up the bells. He said, "I think Happy is buying a lot of clothes and I'm not sure why. What I do know is that isn't the way you should discuss the subject. You might want to ease into it and maybe compliment the clothes and then bring up why she needed them."

Bobby handed Alana the bells and they walked into Tick and Tock's shop. They perused the catalog until she spotted the exact furniture and patio she had seen in the future. As she looked through the pages, Alana thought about Bobby's advice and wondered how she could approach the subject in a better way with Happy. She wanted to help Happy, not hurt her. Alana placed Happy's bells on the counter along with everyone's contributions. Happy's pile of bells was a lot smaller than the others. Alana wanted everyone's share to be equal, and she wanted Happy to realize that what she was doing wasn't fair to the other residents of Furtopia.

Tick and Tock counted the bells, but they were short a few hundred bells. Alana pulled some more from her pocket and handed them to Tick and Tock.

"This is excellent," Tick said. "You are going to have one of the nicest pool patios in the Animal Crossing universe."

The words "I know" almost slipped out of Alana's mouth, but she kept quiet. She didn't want anyone to know that she had traveled to the future.

"We have a week until Lars's party and we need to keep him away from the pool," Bobby said.

"That won't be easy," Tick said. "I think you guys have your work cut out for you. You will have to keep him occupied."

"At least you have the fishing tournament to keep you guys busy," Tock said. "I'm sure you're all preparing for it by practicing all day, right? I'm not participating, but I will be working with D. J. and buying the fish. I can't wait to see who wins. This is the biggest event to ever occur on Furtopia, and I am so excited."

Alana wanted to remind him about the J. J. Swooner concert, but she just said, "I've been practicing a lot, but I don't think I'm going to win. Bobby has been an amazing coach, but I am not the best fisherman. I just hope I don't come in last place."

"It's not about winning or losing," Tock said. "It's about having fun."

Alana listened to Tock's words and tried to believe them.

CHAPTER 12

TRICKS OR CHEATS

O nce the last lounge chair was placed on the patio, Alana planted the orange trees that she knew were going to be full size within the week. Bobby suggested they get back to their training. They didn't have much time to prepare for the contest, but Alana was getting used to the idea that she would come in last. Although this bothered her and kept her up at night with visions of being in last place, she knew that she had to work as hard as she could. She also knew the competition was meant to be fun, and she had to start enjoying practicing. If it was beginning to be a burden, then she told herself she should withdraw from the contest.

Alana looked at the patio and remembered standing at the very foot of the pool minutes before the contest was to begin. It was strange to see the future. Although Alana knew time travel was frowned upon in the Animal Crossing universe, she was curious who won the contest. She should have stuck around to see who was declared the winner. She wanted to go back to hear the winner's name announced. Even though she knew it was a bad idea, the thought had made its way into her mind and wasn't leaving. She wondered if she could go into the future without anyone knowing.

"Alana," Bobby prodded, "your mind seems to be drifting."

"I'm sorry," Alana said. "I was just looking at the patio. I think we did a good job."

"We don't have time to give ourselves compliments. There isn't that much time before the contest." Bobby pulled out his fishing rod and walked to the water. "There's one trick I have yet to tell you and I think this will help you a lot," Bobby said.

"You aren't suggesting I travel to the future again, are you?" Alana joked.

"No," Bobby said, as he pulled bait from his pocket and placed it on the hook. "I made this bait from an oyster I found on the beach. Fish love it and I always win fishing tournaments when I use it."

Alana had read the rule book for the fishing tournament and remembered the rule stating that all contestants must use the same bait. "I thought we had to use the same bait?"

"I know, but if you want, because you're a weaker and more inexperienced fisherman, you can mix this with the bait they provide." Bobby handed some bait to Alana. "Try it."

Alana reluctantly took the bait from Bobby and placed it on her hook. She cast the reel into the water and instantly felt a heavy pull. She reeled in the rod and found two fish hanging from the hook.

"Wow! This really works," Alana said as she pulled the two sea bass from her hook.

Carl walked over to them. "Are you guys practicing? Can I join?"

"Yes," Bobby said.

Carl cast his line and waited for a bite. Alana cast her line and within seconds she felt an even heavier pull. She reeled the line in and found three large sea bass hanging from her hook.

"You certainly improved your fishing skills," Carl remarked. "I think Bobby must be an excellent coach."

"Thanks," Bobby said. "I've been teaching Alana a lot of great tips."

Alana wasn't certain whether Bobby was teaching her tips or cheats. She wanted to confess that she had traveled to the future and watched the contest. She wanted to tell Carl that his bucket was full of fish and that he didn't have to worry, but she didn't want to bring up the fact that she had traveled to the future.

Carl stood by the river for another few minutes and still didn't get a bite. Alana cast her reel again and caught another three fish.

Carl marveled, "How is this happening? I don't get it. How can I get zero bites and you catch three fish at once?"

"I don't know," Alana said. "Luck, I guess."

"Can you teach me any good tips, Bobby?" Carl asked.

"Sure," Bobby said, and he showed Carl how to angle the rod.

Carl felt something and pulled in the line. He pulled a boot from his hook. "This isn't working. I am going to try fishing at the beach. I have better luck there and that's where the contest will take place."

Alana had never seen Carl so energetic. He rushed off to the beach and left Alana and Bobby at the river.

"I should have told Carl about the bait you gave me," Alana said.

"You don't have to use the bait," Bobby said. "I was just trying to help you out."

"It just works so well and now I want to use it, but I feel bad about doing it," Alana explained.

"I get it, but you're also an inexperienced fisherman and it would take you months to reach the same level as everyone else in the competition. I wanted the contest to be fair. If you use the bait, you can instantly improve your skills."

Although what Bobby said made sense, Alana still knew using the bait would be considered cheating. She didn't want to be called out for breaking the rules, but then she didn't want to come in last place either. She didn't know what to do.

"Maybe we should go fish at the beach with Carl?" Alana suggested. She wanted to fish alongside Carl without using the special bait and see how many fish she could catch.

Bobby nodded. "Sounds good."

"And I'm going to fish without the special bait," Alana informed him.

"It's your call," Bobby said.

As they walked toward the beach, they ran into Happy jogging. Alana stopped her.

"I want to apologize for what I said before. Thank you for the bells. We were able to get everything we needed."

"It's okay. I think you're right—I am spending way too much time at the new tailor shop. I think I was just excited because it was something new on the island." Happy looked at Alana's fishing rod. "Are you guys practicing for the competition? Can I join you?"

"Of course," Alana said. She was glad she was able to fish alongside Happy.

CHAPTER 13

DECISIONS

When they reached the shore, they saw Janey, Lars, and Carl having a practice competition. Janey was declared the winner.

"Can we have another one?" Happy asked.

"Of course!" Janey exclaimed. "I love these practice competitions."

"That's because you seem to win every one," Lars said. "I just want to hang out at your place and relax in the hammock."

"No," Alana said, "you have to participate."

"Also, my place is messy," Janey said. "After the competition we should hang out at your place."

Janey's job was to keep Lars away from the pool until the party. It wasn't an easy job, but she had committed to it. Everyone believed Lars was growing suspicious.

"I'd love to practice," Alana said. "Can we start the new practice competition?"

"Yes, let's go," Janey said. "Everyone ready?"

There was a communal yes and Janey started to count down. "One, two, three, begin!"

The gang cast their lines into the sea. Alana decided against using the special bait, and she barely caught any fish. Within the three minutes, she felt about six tugs and reeled in three fish and some garbage.

"Ready to count our fish?" Janey asked.

The gang counted their fish. Carl called out, "I have seven fish. How many do you have, Alana?"

"I have three," Alana replied.

"I told you that I do a much better job fishing in the sea," Carl said with a yawn. Then he excused himself and went to take a nap. Carl didn't stick around to see who had won and to find out that Alana came in last place.

Happy said, "Although Carl isn't here, can we do another practice contest? I'm usually a much better fisherman, but I only caught five fish. I know I could do better than that. I think I've been so preoccupied with the new tailor shop that I haven't been practicing my skills."

Alana had spent the last few weeks practicing, yet she only caught three fish. She decided to use the special bait for this practice competition. She placed the bait on the hook.

"Ready, guys?" Janey asked.

They began. Within seconds, Alana felt a tug on the rod and then another and another. She could barely keep up, and when the contest was over her bucket was overflowing with fish.

"Wow!" Janey exclaimed. "I guess Alana is the winner. We don't even need to count the fish because her bucket is so full."

"That's strange," Happy remarked. "I don't understand how someone can go from last place to first place."

"It happens," Bobby quickly responded.

"You must be the best coach in the universe," Janey said.

"I think I was just lucky," Alana said. "I mean, I did lose the first competition."

Lars suggested, "Let's do one more competition, and then I want to soak in the rays for the remainder of the day."

Janey counted down. Alana cast her line and waited, but nothing bit. In the last minute of the practice competition she was able to reel in one fish.

"This is strange," Happy said. "I don't understand how you won once but came in last twice."

"As I said before, it's luck," Alana replied.

"I hope you're lucky on the day of the competition," Janey said.

Lars said, "Now that the practice games are over, who wants to eat coconuts with me and relax by the water?"

The gang all joined Lars on the beach. Alana liked feeling the warmth of the sun. The summer was ending, and they didn't have much longer to enjoy the lazy days at the beach. As she listened to her friends laugh and tell stories, Alana realized it had been so long since she just had fun. She was so focused on getting Bobby's house built, preparing for Lars's surprise pool party, and endlessly practicing for the fishing competition that she wasn't making time to hang out with her friends. She remembered all the lessons her friends taught her when she was hyper-focused on Furtopia winning the Prettiest Island Award and having J. J. Swooner play a concert on the shore. She promised herself she'd never act like that again, but she was falling into old habits.

Lars asked Alana if she wanted to have a barbecue at his house after the beach, and she said yes. Happy said she'd also join but she wanted to go to the tailor shop first. Alana realized that she and Happy were a lot alike. They both got hyper-focused on different activities. Alana wanted to help Happy because she understood her.

"Do you really need to go to the tailor shop? Can't you just hang out with us? I feel like you're acting the same way I did when I was hyper-focused on Furtopia hosting the J. J. Swooner contest," Alana remarked.

"Am I really acting that way?" Happy asked.

"Kind of," Alana said.

Lars added, "I think you should put shopping on hold for one day and have some fun."

"But I find shopping fun," Happy explained.

"It's a lot more fun hanging out with friends than buying things," Janey said. "I was on my island all by myself and I was so lonely. I was so happy when Lars invited me here. Don't take your friends for granted. You really have to spend time with them. They are more important than filling up your wardrobe with more clothes."

"I guess you're right," Happy said.

"She is right," Lars said.

Alana was talking about the food they were going to cook at the barbecue when she spotted an oyster wash up on the shore. She wanted to point it out to Bobby, so he could pick it up and make some more bait with it. Alana decided not to point out the oyster. She didn't want her friends to question her about it. She had a big decision to make. Would she use the bait or not? Alana decided to put that decision on hold. Tonight, she would have a barbecue with her friends and enjoy the last days of summer.

CHAPTER 14

THE CONTEST

Alana couldn't sleep at all. She tossed and turned all night, but every time she closed her eyes and drifted off to sleep, she'd dream about the fishing competition and would awake in a panic. In one dream, she was catching lots of fish, but when she looked at her bucket, it was empty. In another dream, she stood by the water and didn't get one bite. Alana looked over at her clock. The fishing contest was twenty-four hours away and Alana was worried. She decided to go for a swim in the ocean to relax.

The sun was shining, but there was a slight cool breeze, alerting Alana to the fact that fall was on its way. It was already mid-September and summer was days away from ending. She knew she had to enjoy the last days of swimming at the beach. When she reached the shore, she raced past the waves and dove deep into the water. As she swam, she passed a school of fish, which caused her to think about the competition. There was no escaping the contest. Alana thought about quitting, but she knew her friends would be upset with her. She swam to the shore, got out of the water, and relaxed on the beach. While she soaked in the rays and ate a coconut, Alana spotted another oyster in the wet sand. She picked up the oyster, put it in her pocket, and pulled out her phone. Alana scrolled through the list of DIY recipes on her phone, searching for one that would show her how to make bait. She only had a small amount of Bobby's bait left and she wanted to make sure she had enough for the competition.

Happy came jogging over to the shore. "Alana, are you ready for the contest? I already met D. J. He's on Furtopia preparing for tomorrow's big event!"

"He's here? Wow, that makes it seem even more real," Alana said as she tried to close the bait recipe that was frozen on her screen.

"Is that a recipe for bait?" Happy asked.

"Um, maybe." Alana's face turned red. "I was just looking at the recipe. I wasn't going to use it."

"You know you can't use your own bait in the competition," Happy reminded her.

"I know," Alana said. And then she confessed, "I just don't want to lose."

"You just have to try your hardest, but you can't cheat," Happy explained. "Remember when you told me that I was shopping too much?"

"Yes."

"That really helped me. It made me realize that maybe I was shopping a bit too much. I was just so excited about the shop and the newness of it all that

I didn't realize how many things I was buying. Then I went home and looked through my wardrobe and saw how full it was, and I knew that I had to put a pause on the shopping," Happy admitted. "So now I want to help you. I want you to know that I understand you're nervous about the competition, and everyone knows you're a beginning fisherman, but I can see you're becoming hyper-focused on winning."

"It's not about winning," Alana's said as her eyes swelled with tears. "It's about not coming in last place. Bobby has been coaching me, but it just doesn't seem to work at all!"

"Stop focusing on the outcome. Just focus on enjoying the fun of a competition. Even if you come in last, it will be fine," Happy said.

Alana realized Happy was right. She closed her phone, and when she placed the phone in her pocket, she pulled out the oyster and handed it to Happy. "Please take this. I don't want to be tempted to use it."

Happy smiled. "I know you're going to have fun at the competition."

"I hope so," Alana said.

Just then Janey called out to Alana and Happy. "Guys! I want you to meet D. J."

Although the fishing tournament was to take place the next morning, D. J. was already dressed for the event. He carried a tackle box and wore a waterproof vest, rainboots, and a sun hat.

"I'm so excited to host the event on Furtopia. Thank you for inviting me here, Janey," D. J. said. "It's so nice getting to meet all the contestants before the competition."

"We're so excited to meet you," Happy said. "I've always wanted to be in a fishing competition."

"They are a lot of fun," Janey said.

"Yes," D. J. said. "I've hosted so many competitions and everyone always has a good time."

"What about the ones who come in last place?" Alana asked.

"There's always someone who comes in last. A lot of time a bunch of participants tie for last place," D. J. said. "And there are folks who lose and the next time they enter the competition they win. It's all just good fun."

This comment made Alana feel better and, for the first time, she was actually looking forward to the competition.

The next morning, she awoke early and was one of the first contestants to arrive at the competition.

"Welcome," D. J. greeted her. He stood next to Janey, who was helping him prepare for the competition. Janey and Bobby put the first, second, and third place trophies on a small table. Alana looked at the trophies and wondered if she could win one.

Happy jogged over. "Am I late? I was just trying to get my cardio in before the competition started."

"Nope," D. J. said. "You're right on time."

Lars and Carl strolled over to the shore. Carl yawned and said, "Is there time for a quick nap before the competition starts?"

"I'm afraid not." D. J. looked at his watch. "It's about to begin shortly."

Feathers called out, "Wait for me!"

"Of course," D. J. said.

"And me!" Wayne sprinted to the shore.

Tick and Tock showed up and stood by the trophy table. Tick said, "We will buy the fish you catch."

"We have great prices for fish," Tock added.

"Looks like everything is all set. Get your fishing rods out," D. J. announced. "Let's begin."

Bobby walked over to Alana. "You're going to do a great job," he said. "You worked very hard and you've seriously improved your fishing skills. I'm proud of you."

"Thank you," Alana said.

D. J. started the timer and Alana cast her line into the clear blue ocean water and hoped a fish would bite. She felt a pull, but Alana's palms were sweaty, and the fishing rod almost slipped out of her hand. "At least I caught one fish," Alana thought as she placed the sea bass into her bucket.

CHAPTER 15

COUNTING WHAT YOU CAUGHT

There were two minutes left and Alana had caught three fish. If she kept up at this pace, she would catch nine fish. She looked over at Janey, who pulled two fish off a single hook, and started to panic. It was obvious Janey was going to win, but Alana hoped she wouldn't come in last place. As her heart pounded, Alana took a deep breath and reminded herself to have fun. Once she stopped focusing on what the other contestants were catching or where she placed in the competition, she started to enjoy herself, and Alana even caught two fish at once. She piled the fish into the bucket. When D. J. announced that the competition was over, Alana was shocked to see that her bucket was overflowing with fish.

Alana quickly turned around to see if she could spot her time-traveling self, hiding behind the tree, but she was already gone. She couldn't believe she had traveled into the future to prepare for this competition and that she had contemplated using special bait. She was glad she didn't use the bait.

"Tick and Tock will help me count the fish," D. J. said as he asked everyone to step back from their buckets.

Bobby looked over at Alana's bucket and smiled. "I knew you'd do well."

"I know," Alana said proudly. "I was able to catch all these fish without using the bait."

"See? All you needed to do was practice," Bobby said.

"You were a great coach," Alana replied.

Happy ran over to Alana. "I don't think you came in last place. I saw your bucket and it was so full of fish. I didn't catch too many, but that's okay. You win some, you lose some."

The group waited patiently for the results, but they felt like it was taking an eternity. Alana watched as Tick, Tock, and D. J. pulled the fish from each bucket and counted what everyone had caught.

Feathers walked over to Alana. "Are you planning on selling all of your fish? I ask this because I was hoping you could donate a few to the museum."

"Of course," Alana said, and then asked, "What about the fish you caught?"

"I only caught two and I wanted to have a few more fish in the museum," Feathers replied.

D. J. tallied all the fish and called out, "We will announce the winners."

Everyone crowded around the table that housed the three trophies. D. J. called out, "The third place winner is Lars."

Lars received his trophy and everyone cheered.

"The second place winner is Alana," D. J. announced.

Alana couldn't believe D. J. had called her name. Everyone cheered, but Alana could hear Bobby's voice over the applause. "I knew you could do it," he yelled.

D. J. picked up the first place trophy. "The first place trophy goes to Janey."

As the crowd cheered, Janey took her trophy and said, "Now I'm going to place this on the shelf in my new house. I am so glad I moved to Furtopia. Everyone made me feel so welcome here, and I'm so thankful for that. I also hope this will be the first of many fishing competitions to be held on Furtopia. D. J., do you plan on coming back?"

"Of course! Look at all the skilled fishermen on this island. I'm impressed with each of you. Also the last twenty-four hours on Furtopia has been so much fun. In fact, I'm going to stay for the party."

"What party?" Lars asked.

Alana was shocked that D. J. had mentioned the surprise party. Alana hoped he didn't mention the pool. She hoped they could keep that a surprise, since the party was only a day away.

"The one I plan on throwing tonight to celebrate Janey winning the fishing tournament," D. J. said as he tried to get himself out of trouble.

"Nobody told me about it," Lars said.

"I think we assumed everyone would want to have a celebration. Sorry if I forgot to tell you," Janey said.

"It's going to be a beach party," D. J. said, and then added that they would also do some night fishing.

Feathers remarked, "That's great because I want to get some rare fish for the museum and there's a better chance of catching them at night."

Tick and Tock announced that they were prepared to buy any fish and offer plenty of bells in return. Before Alana sold her fish, she handed three to Feathers. "This is for the museum."

"You are so generous. How can I ever repay you?" Feathers asked.

"There's no need. The museum is one of my favorite places on the island and I just want you to have everything you need to make it the best museum," Alana replied.

"Thank you," Feathers said with a smile.

As the gang sold their fish to Tick and Tock, they found themselves overflowing with bells.

"We're rich!" Happy exclaimed, as she put the shiny new bells in her pocket and said to Alana, "Normally I would have spent all these bells on clothes at the tailor shop, but I think I'm going to save them."

"Maybe you should spend some of these bells on a present for Lars," Alana said in a whisper.

"Good idea! What do you think he wants?" Happy asked.

"Let's go to the store and pick out something for him," Alana suggested.

Alana and Happy walked to the center of town, with Alana clutching her second place trophy with a big smile on her face.

CHAPTER 16

NIGHT FISHING

Alana didn't have time to celebrate with an evening of night fishing and dancing, because she had to get everything ready for Lars's surprise party. Happy, Carl, Bobby, and Janey decided to meet at Alana's house before they went night fishing, to go over the last details.

"How are we going to get Lars over to the pool?" Alana asked.

Janey suggested, "Why don't I have him over for dinner? When he arrives, I'll ask him to take a walk and we'll walk to the pool. We can have everyone at the pool and when we show up, you can all shout 'Surprise!'"

"That sounds like a great plan," Happy said.

"The hard part," Carl said with a yawn, "will be setting everything up without Lars noticing. How are we going to get balloons, a piñata, and a tray full of cupcakes from Alana's house to the pool without Lars noticing?"

"I have an idea," Happy said. "I can ask him to soak in the rays with me at the beach. You know how much

Lars loves the beach. You guys can move everything over to the pool while I'm with Lars."

"This sounds like the best plan ever," Janey said. "I'm so glad I moved to Furtopia and am able to be part of this community. I feel like I have so many best friends here and everyone really cares about each other."

Alana smiled. She was also glad Janey was here. Alana couldn't believe how much she had grown to like Janey. At first, she was jealous of Lars and Janey's friendship, but now she understood that the more friends you had, the better off you were. When they were done planning the last details for the party, the group made their way to the shore for an evening of celebration and night fishing.

When they arrived at the shore, Lars was fishing beside D. J. Lars asked, "Where were you guys? I thought I was the only one who was showing up!"

"Sorry we're late," Janey said, and she pulled out her fishing rod and cast her line into the water.

"We were all a bit tired from the competition," Alana explained.

The sun had set and there was only a faint glow of the moon peeking out from the clouds. She felt a sprinkle of water on her arm. Alana asked, "Did anyone else feel a raindrop?"

"Yes," Happy said. "It's drizzling."

Tick, Tock, and Wayne arrived and were ready to build a big bonfire. Wayne said, "I don't think the bonfire is going to work. The rain will put it out."

Feathers raced toward the water in the dark. "Did you catch anything? Did you find any rare fish?"

"Not yet," Janey said.

The rain began to fall harder and everyone pulled out their rain slickers. "I'm so upset that we can't have a bonfire," D. J. remarked.

The only one who was excited about the rain was Feathers. "You know that you find the rarest and best fish during a night rainstorm. I really hope we catch a coelacanth. So far, I have one in the museum, thanks to Alana, and I'd love to have another one."

Thunder boomed and lighting was seen skimming the water's surface. D. J. suggested they end the night fishing celebration. "I think this might be too dangerous."

"Why doesn't everyone come back to my house and we can celebrate there?" Alana suggested, but then she remembered that her home was filled with all the supplies for Lars's party and regretted inviting everyone.

"That sounds like a great idea!" Happy exclaimed.

Fortunately, at that very moment, the rain stopped. "Wait," Alana said, "I don't feel any raindrops."

"Me neither," Carl said.

The light from the moon lit up the sea as the clouds parted and the rain stopped. Wayne, Tick, and Tock started to make a bonfire on the beach. Avis and Tavis walked over to the group. Avis was carrying a tape deck and she placed it on the sand.

"Anyone up for a dance party?" Tavis asked.

"We wore our party dresses!" Avis exclaimed. Both Tavis and Avis were dressed in purple dresses and wore big bows atop their heads.

"I will dance in a minute," Feathers said as he stood on the shore. "I want to see if I can catch a coelacanth."

Alana walked over to Feathers. "This isn't a time to focus on goals. It's a time to have fun. I promise that I will go night fishing with you at another time and we will try to catch a coelacanth."

Feathers smiled. "You're right. Tonight is a time for celebrations. We just hosted our first fishing tournament and soon D. J. will be leaving to host other tournaments around the universe, and we should enjoy this fun night alongside him."

"That's the spirit!" Alana grabbed his hand and they danced on the sandy beach.

As the clouds parted, more stars appeared in the night sky, illuminating the beach. The gang danced as they celebrated the first fishing competition on Furtopia. Alana wondered what other fun events might happen on this island. She smiled as she danced alongside all of her friends. Tomorrow, they would have a second celebration for Lars's birthday. There was less than twenty-four hours before Lars's party and she hoped they would all be able to keep it a secret until then.

CHAPTER 17

CELEBRATIONS

In the morning, Alana just wanted to stay in bed. She had spent most of the night dancing on the beach with her friends and she didn't have the energy to get up. She still had a lot to do to prepare for Lars's party, but she could barely keep her eyes open. Alana decided to sleep a bit longer and hoped that would do the trick.

She awoke to a knock at her door. She looked over at her clock. It was after eleven, and she still hadn't started on the cupcakes and filled the piñata. She climbed out of bed, and with a yawn, opened the front door.

Lars stood in the doorway. "Alana, do you want to go to the beach with me? I feel like everyone is busy and I am so bored."

"I can't," Alana said. "I'm also busy."

"Why is everyone so busy? What's going on?"

"I think we were all preoccupied with the fishing competition and once that was over, we realized we had a lot of crafting projects and stuff we had put aside. Or at least that's how it is for me. I know Happy wanted to go to the beach."

"Okay, but can you go for a little while? It doesn't have to be for very long. I mean, today is a special day for me," Lars said.

"Yes, it's your birthday," Alana said. She felt bad. She didn't want Lars to think that she had forgotten his birthday.

"I feel like nobody remembered," Lars said with a frown.

"No, I didn't forget. I bought you a hammock."

"Well you didn't wish me a happy birthday when you opened the door. I thought my birthday was going to be more than adequate, but it's turning out to be a disappointment."

Alana didn't know what to say, so she replied, "Let's go to the beach to celebrate your birthday, but I can only stay an hour. We should stop by Happy's first and see if she wants to come."

"Okay, I guess an hour is fine," Lars said.

Alana and Lars didn't have to go to Happy's house, because the minute they stepped onto Alana's front porch, Happy jogged past them.

"Lars! I'm supposed to ask you if you wanted to go to the beach," Happy said as she jogged in place.

"You were supposed to ask me?" Lars was confused.

"I'm sorry, that came out all wrong. What I mean is, do you want to go to the beach with me? Once I finish up my daily cardio, I want to spend the day soaking in the rays and Alana suggested you should go with me because she's busy."

"I'm going to hang out at the beach for a bit because it's Lars's birthday and he wants to spend it at the beach," Alana informed her.

"Happy birthday, Lars! I bought you the best present. I can't wait to give it to you at the—" Happy stopped talking and just jogged in place.

"At the what?" Lars asked.

"At the beach," Happy replied. "I have to go home and get it."

Alana was happy that Lars didn't ask any questions on the walk to the beach. Once they arrived, he picked a spot on the sand near the coconut tree and sat down. "I think I want to hang out here and then go for a swim."

"Do you want a coconut?" Alana asked as she picked one from the tree.

"Of course. It will definitely make my birthday more than adequate." Lars ate the coconut.

As they sat underneath the shady coconut tree, Alana spotted a bottle that had washed up on the shore. She walked over and picked it up. "Lars," Alana called out, "get up. It's your birthday, so you should open the message in the bottle."

Lars got up. He unscrewed the top and took out the note. It said:

Dear Stranger,

I'm sending this to you because it's the most awesome DIY project in the world and I had to share it with you. I've already shared it with all the residents of my amazing island, and they agree this project is super awesome. Here are the directions for making a ukulele.

Signed,
A DIY musician

"I have all the materials to make this!" Alana said. "I'm going to make a ukulele for you. It will be my new birthday present."

"Thank you," Lars said. "I'd love that."

Alana saw Happy jogging toward the beach with a balloon in hand. As she got closer, she began singing "Happy Birthday." When she was finished, she said, "I love that my name is Happy, because when I celebrate birthdays with my friends, it's really a HAPPY birthday." She giggled when she said this and then handed the balloon to Lars.

Lars tied the balloon to the tree. "This is beginning to feel like a birthday party."

When Lars said that Alana realized that she had so many things left to do for the party. "I'm sorry, I have to excuse myself, but I have a lot to do today."

Lars said he understood, and she sprinted home. She was excited to surprise Lars with his big birthday bash at the pool later that day.

CHAPTER 18

ANOTHER YEAR OLDER

When the final cupcake was iced, the ukulele completed, and the piñata filled, Alana carried everything over to the pool. With each step she took to toward the pool, she looked around for Lars. She was finally able to exhale when she reached the pool without being seen. She hung up the piñata and placed the cupcakes on the table.

Janey and Bobby had decorated the area surrounding the pool with streamers and balloons. Carl stacked a pile of party poppers on another table near the barbecue that Wayne, Tick, and Tock were setting up. D. J. placed a bucket of fish next to the barbecue.

"We will be grilling lots of fish tonight," D. J. laughed.

Feathers suggested they clear a space for a bonfire, where they could all hang out after dinner. He chose a spot by the river, which was just steps from the pool.

"I can't wait to dance by the bonfire again tonight. That is so much fun," Feathers said.

Avis and Tavis arrived. They each carried a basket filled with colorful party hats. The sisters handed the party hats out to everyone. "We need to be dressed in festive attire when he arrives."

"When is he arriving?" Carl asked as he sat down by the pool. "I'm getting tired and I don't want this party to go all night. The sooner it gets started, the sooner it will be over."

"It should be any minute now," Janey replied.

Carl picked up the plate of party poppers and handed them out to everyone. "We have to shout 'Surprise!' and then set off our party poppers," Carl instructed everyone. "I love noisemakers because they take very little energy to use, but they create a sense of excitement and celebration."

"That's so true," Feathers agreed.

Janey pulled out a pair of binoculars. "I see them. They're walking over the bridge."

The gang, dressed in party hats with party poppers in hand, crowded behind the orange trees. When they heard Lars ask Happy, "Is that a pool?" they all jumped up and shouted, "Surprise!" and then set off their party poppers.

Lars was in shock. "Wow! You guys are amazing!"

"And you thought we forgot about you," Alana said jokingly.

"We were busy putting together this party," Janey said. "This was all Alana's idea."

"It wasn't mine alone. We all wanted to celebrate

your birthday. Janey thought we should have a pool party, so we got a pool," Alana said.

"This is great! I love pools, and now we have one on Furtopia. This is the best birthday present ever because we can all use this pool together," Lars exclaimed. He walked to the diving board and dove into the pool.

Everyone followed by jumping and diving into the pool. Avis played a tape with J. J. Swooner songs and the gang sang along as they splashed in the new pool.

"This is the best birthday ever," Lars told them. "I can't wait to see what you guys do next year."

Alana laughed. "This party hasn't even ended and you're thinking about next year's party?"

"I'm sorry. I am so happy you guys threw this party for me. Honestly, nobody has ever done anything like this for me before."

The sun set and D. J. announced he had to leave. "I'm sorry to go before it's over, but I'm hosting a competition on another island tomorrow and I have to travel there now."

"Thank you again for hosting the competition," Janey said.

Alana said, "I hope you come back and host another one soon."

"Me too," he replied. Then he turned and walked back to the other side of the island, which housed the dock.

As he walked away, Alana looked up at the stars. She thought about the stars that sprinkled the night sky, and she wondered how many stars there were. It also made her wonder how many islands there were. She wondered how many islands D. J. had visited. He probably knew every island in this island adventure world. She thought about all the messages in bottles she had picked up since she had arrived on Furtopia and bet that D. J. had met all of those strangers who had sent their DIY projects out to sea. Or perhaps the messages were all sent from one person. Alana wanted to travel to find out who sent them. She also hoped she'd meet more folks who might want to live on Furtopia, like Janey and Bobby. She couldn't wait to see who else would move to the island. There was a great big world out there, and she wanted to explore it. For now, she was happy enjoying this festive event with her friends.

Alana pulled out the ukulele she had made from the directions given to her by a stranger. At the start of the summer, Lars was a stranger, and now he was one of her best friends. She handed him the ukulele, and he surprised everyone by playing a J. J. Swooner ballad. The song was about a dog who longed to be free and travel the world. Alana listened to Lars do his best J. J. Swooner impersonation as he lowered his voice and crooned the heartfelt melody.

Everyone applauded when the song ended. Lars bowed and then pointed. "I see a piñata! Let's play!"

The gang each took turns wearing a blindfold and hitting the piñata until it burst open, showering them with candy. Everyone grabbed what they could and filled their pockets with sweets.

At the end of the night, Alana put a candle in one of the cupcakes and the group sang "Happy Birthday." Then Lars blew out his candle.

"I hope you made a wish," Alana said.

"It already came true," Lars smiled.

ALSO AVAILABLE

WELCOME TO

FURTOPIA

AN UNOFFICIAL NOVEL FOR
FANS OF ANIMAL CROSSING

ISLAND
ADVENTURES
BOOK #1

WINTER MORGAN
NATIONAL BESTSELLING AUTHOR